Fiesta!

NO matter where you might be in Spain, a fiesta is probably not too far away. One of the most famous fiestas is the Fiesta de San Fermin in the northern city of Pamplona. The central event of this fiesta is the Running of the Bulls, when daring participants run before a herd of bulls being driven from their corrals to the Plaza de Toros, or bullring. This event celebrates the opening of the bullfighting season in Spain. Valencia, on the east coast of Spain, holds a week-long fiesta each year celebrating Saint Joseph's Day. The centerpiece of the festival is the burning of hundreds of *fallas*, or floats, following a spectacular parade. The largest fiesta in Spain is the solemn religious celebration of Semana Santa, or Holy Week, held in the southern city of Seville. Following the Semana Santa by two weeks is the Feira de Abril, or the April Fair, which features horse shows, bullfights, and flamenco dancing.

Song and Dance

SONG and dance are part of most Spanish fiestas and other celebrations. Flamenco is a kind of Spanish song and dance accompanied by heel clicking, hand clapping, finger snapping, and shouting. It is believed to have originated with the Gypsies of southern Spain. Two other popular forms of song and dance are the bolero and the fandango. In both these dances the dancers use castanets, wooden disks held in the hand and clapped together. These dances may also be accompanied by guitar and tambourine.

Fiesta Brava—The Bullfight

WE may know it as the bullfight, but to the Spanish it is *la fiesta brava*, or brave festival. Bullfighting is very popular throughout the Spanish-speaking world, but nowhere more than in Spain. In a bullfight event, or *corrida*, three *matadors* each fight two bulls. Each contest between *matador* and bull lasts about twenty minutes and ends with the death of the bull.

Matadors, or *matadoras* as women bullfighters are called, wear a silk jacket embroidered in gold, tight pants, and a two-horned hat. A red cape is waved before the bull to encourage him to charge in the direction of the matador.

US REGIONS OF SPAIN

XTREMADURA   GALICIA   LA RIOJA   MADRID   MURCIA   NAVARRA   PAÍS VASCO   VALENCIA

Following Isabella

Written by Linda Talley

Illustrated by Andra Chase

MarshMedia, Kansas City, Missouri

To Aunt Dorothy and Uncle Randall.

Published by

A Division of Marsh Film Enterprises, Inc.
P. O. Box 8082
Shawnee Mission, KS 66208

Library of Congress Cataloging-in-Publication Data
Talley, Linda.
    Following Isabella / written by Linda Talley; illustrated by Andra Chase.
        p.   cm.
    Summary: Isabella the sheep sets out to become a leader and ultimately saves the flock from a deadly wildfire. Includes nonfiction information about Spain.
    ISBN 1-55942-163-0
    [1. Sheep—Fiction. 2. Spain—Fiction] I. Chase, Andra, ill. II. Title.
PZ7.T156355Fo 2000   00-060945
[E]—dc21

Book layout and typography by Cirrus Design

Special thanks to Roberto Agnolini,
Bud Dean, and Wesley Solski.

Printed in Hong Kong

*I*f you look at a map of Spain, you will see what some people think looks like the stretched out hide of a bull. Well, the Spanish love bullfighting, so maybe that notion is just the power of suggestion at work. In any case, looking at your map, you will see in the north the lofty Cantabrian Mountains and the great Pyrenees that separate Spain and France. Then a little further south, you will see, snaking across your map, first the Ebro River, which flows east into the Mediterranean, then the Douro River, which flows west through Portugal into the Atlantic.

But come back. Don't follow either of those rivers, please. Instead, continue southward and locate on your map the historic town of Segovia. Yes, right there, above the Sierra de Guadarrama, in the Meseta, the very heart of Spain.

Now, not far from Segovia—none of this last will be on your map, of course—lies a little village of two hundred souls, and outside the village is a farm. On this farm, in the shade of a few evergreen oaks, stands a flock of sheep, among them one named Isabella.

Isabella is the hero of our story.

Isabella is a most amiable ewe. She never disagrees with anyone. She never demands her own way. As Isabella and the other sheep in the flock graze the countryside, she is content to trail along behind whoever happens to be a few steps ahead of her.

Of course, the same could be said for every other sheep in the flock, be it María or Carlos or Milagros or Rocío or Antonio. Being sheep, they have a natural inclination to follow.

Oh, there have been exceptions to this rule. One ancient ram, Pedro, was once a leader.

In those days, when Pedro called out "Follow me!" the other sheep knew they would soon be grazing on the greenest hillside or drinking from the coolest stream or resting beneath the shadiest oaks.

Pedro also steered the flock clear of trouble. If the lambs wandered near a stream swollen by a spring torrent, he nudged them along to a safe place.

If the flock drifted toward the poisonous weed that sprang up at certain times of the year, Pedro called out a warning.

But now Pedro is—well, old—slow on his feet and nearly blind. The flock has no leader. The sheep drift along with their heads to the ground. Then, sooner or later, one of them, say Milagros, wanders off in her own direction.

"Ah," María calls out to the others, "Milagros smells tender wild rosemary. I can tell by the way she hurries along!" When the flock has followed Milagros halfway to Madrid, or so it seems to Isabella, Antonio heads off in a new direction.

"Ah," Carlos says, "Antonio has caught the scent." They are all soon on Antonio's heels. But Antonio slackens, and Rafaela suddenly hurries off yet another way.

Through all this, Isabella follows along with the others, thinking that the rosemary grows on a hill behind the farmhouse, not down this rocky path.

Finally they find themselves in a dry and gravelly gully, staring at each other with wide eyes, not a sprig of rosemary in sight.

"Rosemary?" protests Milagros. "I was just looking for a spot of shade!"

"I was thirsty and was heading for the stream!" Antonio says.

"A wasp was after me!" Rafaela explains.

Well, this is the way things had been going for some time, when one day Isabella stomped her hoof in exasperation.

"Why must we always be wandering about willy-nilly, nobody knowing where we are going?" she asked. "We are as likely to end up on a rock pile as in green pasture. Things must have worked much more smoothly in the old days when Pedro was leading the flock."

The others stared at her in amazement.

"Isabella," Pedro laughed, "I am too old and bleary-eyed to lead the flock. *You* are such a clever sheep. Perhaps another day, *you* can lead us to where the wild rosemary grows."

The very next day, as the little flock was grazing, Isabella called out to them, "If anyone would care to follow me, I think I know where there is a bit of tender rosemary growing." And with that, she set off for the hill behind the farmhouse.

Not halfway there, Antonio veered off in another direction. The flock drifted after him. "No!" Isabella called out firmly. "The rosemary is this way. Follow me!" The others hesitated.

"Let's give Isabella a chance to lead us," said Pedro.

So the whole flock turned and followed Isabella to the spot on the hill where the rosemary grew. They all bleated their appreciation.

"You did it, Isabella!" said Pedro. "You did it!"

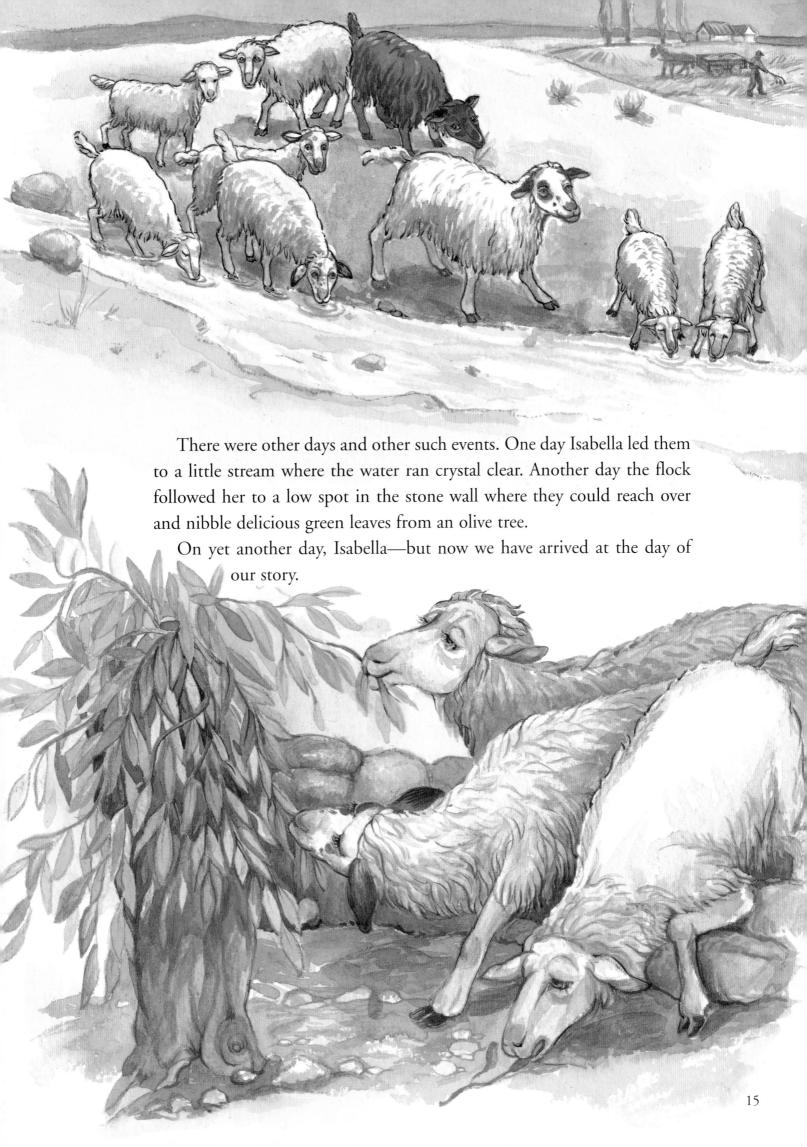

There were other days and other such events. One day Isabella led them to a little stream where the water ran crystal clear. Another day the flock followed her to a low spot in the stone wall where they could reach over and nibble delicious green leaves from an olive tree.

On yet another day, Isabella—but now we have arrived at the day of our story.

Late summer had arrived and with it drought. The little streams had gone dry, and the grass was brittle and tasteless. The flock had spent the better part of the day huddled in the shade of the oaks.

Then, late in the afternoon, big puffs of white clouds billowed up behind the Alcazar at Segovia.

"Unless I'm mistaken," said Pedro, sniffing the air, "there is rain on the way. And perhaps something more." Isabella smiled at the thought of big fat raindrops falling on the dusty ground, of sweet water sinking down to feed the roots of the grass, and of the clear, bright air that would follow the rain. But she felt uneasy over Pedro's last words. What else might the clouds bring?

The billowing clouds grew, blocking the blistering sun. Isabella and the flock ventured out from the canopy of oaks and spread over the field, happy to be able to graze without the hot sun on their backs. They drifted along, scarcely lifting their heads as they looked for any green thing spared by the drought.

The wind came up so quickly.

When Isabella raised her head in alarm, dust blew into her eyes. Then she saw that the white clouds had disappeared. Now an enormous greenish-black cloud filled the western sky and rolled toward the sheep. The storm was upon them.

Thunder crashed. Lightning cracked the sky in two. Isabella worried that it might crack the earth in two also. Then a tremendous bolt of lightning struck the dry field. The flock panicked. They scattered in every direction.

Then Isabella saw it—smoke boiling up from over the hill.
A wildfire raged, sparked by the lightning.

Without thinking, Isabella called out, "Don't run! Follow
me!" She turned to Pedro with panic in her eyes. Which way?

"Isabella," he said, "you must find the way home!"

She thought quickly. They could run to the lane, where there was little grass to burn—follow it to the farm. Surely that was the best way. Or was it? Perhaps they should follow the streambed—keep low. Oh, what if she chose the wrong way?

But even as she was thinking, smoke billowed around the flock. Isabella could see only a few feet ahead. How could she find the lane *or* the streambed? Isabella wished with all her heart that there was someone to tell her which way to go.

She heard the little thumps of hooves as the flock huddled around her. Then she saw Milagros head away from the flock.

"Milagros must know the way," Isabella sighed hopefully. Maybe Milagros would lead them out. Isabella might not have to decide after all.

The flock started off behind Milagros. Last of all trailed Isabella. She had been eager to follow Milagros at first, but with every step she became more uncertain. "How does Milagros know the way?" she worried.

Just then, a gust of wind cleared the smoke above Isabella.

She could see the Alcazar high above the plain. Milagros was leading them in the wrong direction! Away from the farm!

"WAIT!" she called out. "That's not the way to go! FOLLOW ME!"

The others turned. They hesitated.

"Follow me!" called Isabella again.

Now Isabella had her bearings. She turned around and headed in the direction where she knew they must cross the lane.

"Follow Isabella!" the others called out.

And they did follow Isabella, across gullies and fields to the lane and then down the lane to the farm. Isabella led the flock safely home. Just as they entered the farmyard, the clouds burst and the rain poured down.

Isabella ran to the shelter of the barn. From beneath its eaves she watched the big fat raindrops falling and sniffed the fresh clear air.

You won't be surprised to hear that the rest of Isabella's flock did just the same!

Dear Parents and Educators:

Among the greatest leaders are those who are dedicated to serving their fellow citizens. We are indebted to those honest and caring leaders who make a daily decision to try to make life less difficult for others. They model for us that personal happiness is really the by-product of improving the circumstances of others and that contentment and success come from giving, not getting.

There are many kinds of leaders and many styles of leadership. Some lead with public displays of bravado, while others inspire more quietly. Some step forward to lead during times of crisis. Others lead by steady example and commitment. Leadership requires a level of effort and energy that is more than some of us are willing to muster, but we are lucky enough to have dedicated people who come forward to lead community groups or to help organize and direct others within their workplaces. Creative and imaginative leaders help us chart new territory and teach us to stretch beyond our comfort zone to new and exciting opportunities. Special gifts and talents may make some people especially suited for leadership roles, but most skills needed for effective leadership can be learned.

Being a leader in any capacity is a demanding yet rewarding role. In educating our young people today, we strive to develop their confidence, courage, and initiative so that they will be willing and able to take on leadership roles. We also try to develop the skills children need to be good followers, proud to take on a subordinate role when the situation calls for support.

Encourage children to share their ideas and feelings about Isabella's experiences. Here are some questions to help initiate discussion about the message of *Following Isabella*.

- Are sheep usually leaders or followers?
- How did Isabella behave at the beginning of the story?
- Did the flock need a leader? Why?
- What caused Isabella to take on a leadership role?
- Did the flock want to follow Isabella at first?
- What happened to the flock during the storm?
- Was Isabella confident that she could lead the other sheep home?
- How do you think Isabella felt about herself at the end of the story?
- Have you ever been a leader in your family? With your friends?
- Are leaders helpers?
- How does helping others make you feel?

Work to create a supportive environment in your home or classroom, where children learn about the responsibilities and rewards of leadership and practice the skills necessary to become leaders.

- Give children age appropriate chores and responsibilities.
- Help children understand the need for rules and boundaries.
- Create opportunities for children to serve others in the community.
- Compliment initiative and creativity in children.
- Encourage children to set goals and to take calculated risks.
- Help children practice making decisions and resolving conflicts.
- Praise children for respectfully standing up for their rights and the rights of others.

Available from MarshMedia

These storybooks, each hardcover with dust jacket and full-color illustrations throughout, are available at bookstores, or you may order by calling MarshMedia toll free at 1-800-821-3303.

Amazing Mallika, written by Jami Parkison, illustrated by Itoko Maeno. 32 pages. ISBN 1-55942-087-1.

Bailey's Birthday, written by Elizabeth Happy, illustrated by Andra Chase. 32 pages. ISBN 1-55942-059-6.

Bastet, written by Linda Talley, illustrated by Itoko Maeno. 32 pages. ISBN 1-55942-161-4.

Bea's Own Good, written by Linda Talley, illustrated by Andra Chase. 32 pages. ISBN 1-55942-092-8.

Clarissa, written by Carol Talley, illustrated by Itoko Maeno. 32 pages. ISBN 1-55942-014-6.

Emily Breaks Free, written by Linda Talley, illustrated by Andra Chase. 32 pages. ISBN 1-55942-155-X.

Feathers at Las Flores, written by Linda Talley, illustrated by Andra Chase. 32 pages. ISBN 1-55942-162-2.

Following Isabella, written by Linda Talley, illustrated by Andra Chase. 32 pages. ISBN 1-55942-163-0.

Gumbo Goes Downtown, written by Carol Talley, illustrated by Itoko Maeno. 32 pages. ISBN 1-55942-042-1.

Hana's Year, written by Carol Talley, illustrated by Itoko Maeno. 32 pages. ISBN 1-55942-034-0.

Inger's Promise, written by Jami Parkison, illustrated by Andra Chase. 32 pages. ISBN 1-55942-080-4.

Jackson's Plan, written by Linda Talley, illustrated by Andra Chase. 32 pages. ISBN 1-55942-104-5.

Jomo and Mata, written by Alyssa Chase, illustrated by Andra Chase. 32 pages. ISBN 1-55942-051-0.

Kiki and the Cuckoo, written by Elizabeth Happy, illustrated by Andra Chase. 32 pages. ISBN 1-55942-038-3.

Kylie's Concert, written by Patty Sheehan, illustrated by Itoko Maeno. 32 pages. ISBN 1-55942-046-4.

Kylie's Song, written by Patty Sheehan, illustrated by Itoko Maeno. 32 pages. (Advocacy Press) ISBN 0-911655-19-0.

Minou, written by Mindy Bingham, illustrated by Itoko Maeno. 64 pages. (Advocacy Press) ISBN 0-911655-36-0.

Molly's Magic, written by Penelope Colville Paine, illustrated by Itoko Maeno. 32 pages. ISBN 1-55942-068-5.

My Way Sally, written by Mindy Bingham and Penelope Paine, illustrated by Itoko Maeno. 48 pages. (Advocacy Press) ISBN 0-911655-27-1.

Papa Piccolo, written by Carol Talley, illustrated by Itoko Maeno. 32 pages. ISBN 1-55942-028-6.

Pequeña the Burro, written by Jami Parkison, illustrated by Itoko Maeno. 32 pages. ISBN 1-55942-055-3.

Plato's Journey, written by Linda Talley, illustrated by Itoko Maeno. 32 pages. ISBN 1-55942-100-2.

Tessa on Her Own, written by Alyssa Chase, illustrated by Itoko Maeno. 32 pages. ISBN 1-55942-064-2.

Thank You, Meiling, written by Linda Talley, illustrated by Itoko Maeno. 32 pages. ISBN 1-55942-118-5.

Time for Horatio, written by Penelope Paine, illustrated by Itoko Maeno. 48 pages. (Advocacy Press) ISBN 0-911655-33-6.

Toad in Town, written by Linda Talley, illustrated by Itoko Maeno. 32 pages. ISBN 1-55942-165-7.

Tonia the Tree, written by Sandy Stryker, illustrated by Itoko Maeno. 32 pages. (Advocacy Press) ISBN 0-911655-16-6.

Companion videos and activity guides, as well as multimedia kits for classroom use, are also available. MarshMedia has been publishing high-quality, award-winning learning materials for children since 1969. To order or to receive a free catalog, call 1-800-821-3303, or visit us at www.marshmedia.com.

The Kingdom of Spain

MOST of the Kingdom of Spain is located on the Iberian Peninsula in western Europe. The Balearic Islands, in the Mediterranean, and the Canary Islands, off the coast of Africa in the Atlantic Ocean, are also part of Spain and make up two of Spain's seventeen autonomous regions.

Almost half of Spain is a huge, dry plateau in the central part of the country. This plateau, or tableland, is called the Meseta. Here the weather is consistently dry and sunny, but the temperature varies from fiercely hot in the summer to bitterly cold in the winter. When drought sets in, which is not uncommon, the landscape turns brown and a haze called the *calina* often hangs in the air. The occasional thunderstorm is welcome. Madrid, Spain's capital and largest city, is located in the Meseta.

Spain is a country of varied languages, landscapes, and customs, but no matter where we travel in Spain we will find castles, churches, fiestas, bullfights, and music.

The Castles of Spain

A castle is a fortified stronghold, usually built to protect kings, queens, and nobility from invading enemies. The earliest castles of Europe were built of wood. Later, after about 1100, they were built of stone. With walls up to thirty feet thick, many of these ancient castles are still standing.

Spain has over 2,500 castles. Perhaps the most famous, certainly the most photographed, is the Alcazar, which stands within the ancient town walls of Segovia. Isabella I, the Spanish queen who sent Christopher Columbus to the Americas, once made her home in this castle.

The Churches of Spain

SOME of the world's most beautiful churches and cathedrals are found in Spain. The cathedral at Seville is the third largest in Europe. Since the Middle Ages, pilgrims have traveled to the Cathedral at Santiago de Compostela, in northern Spain, where the bones of Saint James the Great, a saint especially venerated in Spain, are believed to be buried. Now the entire town, including the famous cathedral, has been made into a national monument. Perhaps the most unusual church in Spain is the Church of the Holy Family in the city of Barcelona. Construction of this church was begun in 1884 and continues today!

THE FLAGS OF THE AUTON

ANDALUCÍA   ARAGÓN   ASTURIAS   BALEARES   CANARIAS   CANTABRIA   CASTILLA-LA MANCHA   CASTILLA Y LEÓN   CATA